W9-AHN-704

Let's Play Tag!

- Read the Page
- ▶ Read the Story
- ★ Game
- ☺ Yes ☹ No
- ↻ Repeat
- ■ Stop

Once upon a time a princess named Rapunzel was born. Rapunzel was a very special girl whose magical hair had the power to heal the sick and injured, and could keep people from growing old.

Mother Gothel, a vengeful old woman who wanted to remain forever young, stole the princess and locked her away in a tower. To keep Rapunzel from leaving, the woman told her the world outside was full of danger and horrible, selfish people.

Rapunzel found lots of ways to pass the time. And when a day seemed to drag—doing the same things over and over—she'd think to herself, "Oh, come on, it's not that bad."

But each year on her birthday, when she saw thousands of floating lights fill the sky, she longed to know what things were like out there.

Then one day, when Mother Gothel was away on a trip, Rapunzel had the chance to find out.

Flynn Rider, a young thief on the run from the palace guards, climbed in through Rapunzel's window.

"Alone at last," Flynn said to himself.

PANG! Rapunzel knocked him out with a frying pan. She hid Flynn's bag of stolen goods, and, when he woke up, struck a deal with him.

"Take me to see the floating lights—"

Flynn interrupted. "You mean the lantern thing they do for the missing princess?"

Rapunzel nodded. "And after you bring me home safely, I'll return your satchel."

Flynn did want his things back. "Fine, I'll take you."

Outside the tower, the world was full of wonders. It was nothing like Mother Gothel had described.

"This is so fun!" Rapunzel shouted. Then she paused. "Mother would be so furious."

Flynn reassured her. "A little rebellion, a little adventure, that's good. Healthy, even."

"You think?" Rapunzel said.

"I know," said Flynn.

WANTED!
By Order of The KING
1000 CROWNS REWARD

Flynn Ryder
THIEF

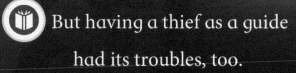 But having a thief as a guide
had its troubles, too.

A lot of people—including Mother Gothel—
were searching for Flynn. To escape, Flynn
and Rapunzel ran through a dark cavern
and swam through an underwater tunnel.
Rapunzel's magical hair glowed,
lighting their way.

M other Gothel failed to stop them, and Rapunzel and Flynn arrived at the Kingdom. It was beyond anything Rapunzel had imagined. She and Flynn had the best day, ever.

That night, they watched the lanterns lit for the missing princess soar into the sky.

"I don't know what it is, but I feel like I belong here," Rapunzel said.

But, Mother Gothel found them and tricked Rapunzel into thinking that the only reason Flynn helped her was to get back his satchel.

Mother Gothel brought Rapunzel back to the tower.

The next day, Rapunzel started thinking about the things she'd seen, and the way the lanterns were always released on her birthday. It was as if . . .

Rapunzel gasped.

"I'm the lost princess!"

She confronted Mother Gothel, who confessed to kidnapping Rapunzel when she was a baby.

Rapunzel left Mother Gothel and the tower for good, and returned to her true family—the King and Queen. She was reunited with Flynn, too.

Soon, a grand celebration was held. And they all lived happily ever after.

handsome perfect round

cute wild bright

ugly crazy dangerous

scary greasy beady

dark green small

bulbous blue huge

WANTED!

FLYNN RIDER

Rider is a very _____ thief with _____ eyes,

a nose that's _____, and _____ hair.

Rider can easily escape any _____ situation.

He was last spotted dashing through the forest.

All who encounter Rider should consider him

_____ and _____.